THE DAY DEATH DIED

Published by Barrington Stoke
An imprint of HarperCollins*Publishers*
1 Robroyston Gate, Glasgow, G33 1JN

www.barringtonstoke.co.uk

HarperCollins*Publishers*
Macken House, 39/40 Mayor Street Upper,
Dublin 1, DO1 C9W8, Ireland

First published in 2025

ISBN 978-0-00-876489-0

10 9 8 7 6 5 4 3 2 1

A catalogue record for this book is available from the British Library

Printed and bound in India by Replika Press Pvt. Ltd.

This book contains FSC™ certified paper and other controlled sources to ensure responsible forest management.

For more information visit: www.harpercollins.co.uk/green

THE DAY DEATH DIED

Tanya Landman

Illustrated by
CINTHYA ÁLVAREZ

Barrington Stoke

To Rod, who told this story so brilliantly

Jack and his mum lived by the sea.

Mum was ill. Each day, she got worse. She got thin. Went to bed early. She got up later and later.

One morning, she didn't get up at all.

There was a knock at the door. Who could it be?

"I've come for your mum," the stranger said.

Jack knew the stranger. It was Death.

“No!” yelled Jack. “No! No! You’re not taking her!”

Jack grabbed a broom and hit Death hard. Again. Again!

It was very odd. Each time Jack hit Death, Death got smaller. And smaller. And smaller.

Until he was so small, Jack could squash him into an empty jam jar!

Jack screwed on the lid.

He ran across the beach and threw the jar far out to sea.

It bobbed away, over the water.

Jack went home.

Mum was up! Smiling. Looking well.

"I'm hungry," she said. "I'll cook us some egg and chips. Pull up some potatoes, Jack. Pick some peas. I'll fry the eggs."

But the eggs wouldn't break.

Jack couldn't pull the potatoes out of the ground. The peas wouldn't come off their stalks.

"How about roast chicken instead?" asked Mum.

But they couldn't kill the chicken.

"I'll go to the shop," Jack said.

Jack walked to the village. There were a lot of angry people standing in the street because there was no meat in the butcher's. No fish in the fish shop. No fruit, no vegetables.

There was no food to buy because nothing could die.

Jack knew he had to get Death back. Then people would have food to eat.

He walked along the beach. Over the cliffs. To the next beach. Day after day. Night after night.

Then he crossed oceans. Deserts. Mountains. He couldn't find Death.

But Jack found war. Famine. Disease. People, animals – all suffering, all wanting to die. But they couldn't.

Jack walked and walked until at last he was home again.

And then he saw his jar, bobbing in the sea ...

Jack opened the jar. Death whooshed out.

"I'm very sorry," said Jack. "I didn't know we needed you. Do you have to take my mum away?"

"One day," said Death. "But not just yet. There's an awful lot of work to catch up on first. It might be a while."

And it was.

Jack's mum lived a very long, very happy life. She was old and tired, and when Death came calling for her, she was happy to go with him.

Jack was sad to see her go but knew it was time. He'd learned his lesson.

Without Death, there is no Life.

Our books are tested
for children and young people by
children and young people.

Thanks to everyone who consulted on
a manuscript for their time and effort in
helping us to make our books better
for our readers.